This book belongs to

_____

ALL IN A DAY'S WORK

CONSTRUCTION WORKER WANTED

TEACHER WANTED

FIRE-FIGHTER WANTED

POLICE OFFICER WANTED

POSTAL WORKER WANTED

Disney's

READ and GROW LIBRARY

Published by Advance Publishers
Winter Park, Florida

Written by Sharon Shavers Gayle   Edited by Bonnie Brook
Penciled by Don Williams   Painted by H.R. Russell
Designed by Design Five
Cover art by Peter Emslie
Cover design by Irene Yap

ISBN: 1-885222-91-2
10 9 8 7 6 5 4 3 2 1

One morning, on his way to work, Donald Duck paused to look in the window of the Duckburg Jewelry Store. He wanted to get another peek at the necklace he planned to buy for Daisy Duck for her birthday.

Donald gazed at the necklace for a long time before he glanced at his watch. "Wak!" he said. "I'm late for work!"

When Donald arrived at the office, Uncle Scrooge was waiting for him. "This is the fourth time this week you've been late," said Uncle Scrooge. "You're fired!"

Donald started to explain why he was late, but Uncle Scrooge wouldn't listen. Sadly, Donald cleaned out his desk and left.

Back at Donald's house, Huey, Dewey, and Louie were getting ready for school.

"Fired again?" said Huey.

"That's the tenth time this year," said Dewey.

"I know, I know," Donald moaned.

"Don't worry," said Louie. "You'll think of something. You always do."

"Yeah," Huey added. "There are lots of jobs."

Suddenly Donald cheered up. "You're right, boys. I'll walk you to school, and then I'll find a new job."

Donald was just leaving his nephews' school when suddenly Daisy Duck, the principal, grabbed him.

"Wak!" said Donald. "I know—your birthday is next week. I didn't forget!"

"No, no," said Daisy. "I need your help. One of our teachers is sick, and we need a substitute."

"It's your lucky day!" said Donald. "I just happen to be available for the job! As a matter of fact, I did very well at school—"

"I'm sure you did," said Daisy. "Now, please, just get in there and bring that classroom under control."

Donald walked into the classroom. A dozen paper airplanes whizzed past him. He picked up a math book. "Aw, phooey!" he said. "Too many numbers."

Then he picked up a spelling book. "Too many letters!"

"Uh—class?" Donald yelled. "Quiet please!"

The students kept yelling and playing.

"Achoo!" came a sound from behind Donald. It was the class's real teacher. In an instant, the students became quiet and sat upright in their seats.

"Glad you're feeling better, sir," said Donald as he hurried out of the room.

Donald was walking out of the school wondering what kind of job he could get next when his pal Gyro Gearloose drove by in his latest invention—a new kind of sanitation truck.

"Hey, Donald," said Gyro, "any chance you can help me pick up the trash today?"

"You're one lucky guy!" said Donald. "I just happen to be available for the job. As a matter of fact, I'm extremely neat by nature—"

"Great!" said Gyro. "Hop in!"

"Now," Gyro explained as he drove the new truck. "The sanitation department likes to have the trash picked up as quickly and neatly as possible. That way, we can keep our city clean!

"I invented this little contraption to do just that. Just push the button, and trash will fly into the truck."

Gyro got out next to a trash can while Donald pushed the button. The trash flew all right. All over Gyro.

"Oops," said Donald. "Sorry about that, Gyro."

To himself, he thought it was time for a new job.

Suddenly Donald spotted a fire in front of the pancake house. He raced to call the fire department.

Seconds later, the fire engine arrived.

"They look as if they could use my help," thought
Donald.

Quickly, he ran to attach one end of the hose to the
fire hydrant. Then he pointed the hose toward the fire
as the firefighter turned on the water.

Donald thought he was ready, but when the water came on, the powerful stream flipped him upside down! Donald put out the fire, but he soaked the firefighters, too.

"Sorry," said Donald. "I was just trying to help."

"Fire hoses are powerful. We go through a lot of training to learn to use them," said one of the firefighters. "But you were very brave."

"Really?" said Donald. "You know, I just happen to be available for a job if you need extra help—"

"I'm afraid we don't right now," the firefighter said.

Donald walked sadly away.

Outside the post office, Donald spotted Goofy, dressed in his postal uniform, ready to deliver mail.

"Hi, Goofy!" said Donald. "I don't suppose the post office is looking for workers?"

"Gawrsh, Donald. We sure are. We need mail sorters right away!"

Inside the post office, Donald was handed a new uniform and told to get to work. "Yikes!" he said looking at the piles of letters in front of him. "Where did all this mail come from?"

Donald was told to sort all the mail into different
stacks. It was quite a job! When he was finished,
Donald's supervisor asked him to help load the sacks of
mail onto the mail truck.

Donald finished loading the truck just before it had to leave on its delivery route.

Suddenly pieces of mail started to fly through the air. "Wak! I forgot to close the door on the mail truck! I think I'd better find a different job—one that's just right for me!"

After Donald left the post office, he noticed that cars were moving very slowly on the street. As he rounded a corner, he saw that a traffic light was out. Traffic was backing up.

"I've always wanted to be a policeman," Donald said.

In the middle of the intersection, Donald pointed to the first car. "Go this way!" he said.

"Go that way!" he said to the next car.

This way, that way, that way, this way. With Donald directing traffic, the drivers didn't know which way to turn.

"Here, let me help you," Donald heard a voice behind him. It was police chief Law Norder. Together, they cleared the traffic.

"Say, chief," Donald said. "It looks as if you may need some help on this corner. You know, I just happen to be available for the job—"

"Sorry, Donald," said the chief. "We just hired some new cadets from the police academy. They've gone through a lot of training to learn to be police officers. But I hear they may be looking for help at the hospital."

"Thanks, Chief!" said Donald as he hurried off.

As Donald walked along, he thought of how important hospitals were to the community. Doctors and nurses not only took care of sick people, but also tried to keep people healthy.

"I'm sure they could use my help," thought Donald.

Donald was lucky. The hospital had an opening for
the very important job of orderly.

"Now, Donald," said Clarabelle Cow, the head nurse,
"before you get your training, we need you to return
these flowers to the flower shop and show this visitor to
the waiting room."

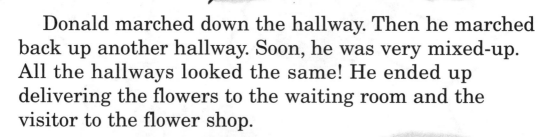

Donald marched down the hallway. Then he marched back up another hallway. Soon, he was very mixed-up. All the hallways looked the same! He ended up delivering the flowers to the waiting room and the visitor to the flower shop.

"This isn't quite working out, Donald," said Clarabelle. "Orderlies go through a lot of training before they can do their job well. But don't worry. You'll find something."

Donald wasn't worried. He already had his eyes on the construction site across the street.

As Donald crossed the street to the construction site, he saw a sign that read:

Construction Workers Wanted

"Oh, boy! Look at all those neat machines!" said Donald. "I've always wanted to be a construction worker."

The construction site foreman looked busy, so Donald decided to hop on the bulldozer and start working. Trying to look like a good worker, Donald eagerly pushed away mounds of dirt.

Donald didn't realize he was headed toward a group of other workers.

Donald was just beginning to wonder which lever might work the brakes on the bulldozer when he accidentally scooped up all the other workers.

"I guess driving bulldozers requires more training, too," thought Donald as he ran down the street.

"Hey, Donald," called Horace Horsecollar. Horace was a worker for the telephone company. "Hop in. We're having a problem with some telephone lines. I could use help fixing them."

When they arrived at the scene, Donald eagerly raced up the telephone pole. "Leave it to me," he said.

"Be careful!" cried Horace. "That's dangerous."

Donald started disconnecting and reconnecting all sorts of wires. Then he looked down. Way down. "Wak! It's high up here!" he said, wobbling. He grabbed onto the pole, tangling himself in the wires.

Meanwhile, Uncle Scrooge had his own problems. Paperwork was piling up on his desk, his coffee had spilled, and he couldn't remember any of his appointments. Now, his phone was ringing off the hook, and when he answered, he kept getting strangers who had dialed the wrong number!

"I need Donald back," he sighed.

A little while later, Huey, Dewey, and Louie spotted Donald walking toward home.

"Boys," said Donald, feeling very tired, "I don't think I'll be able to get Daisy her birthday gift after all. I can't seem to find the right job."

"We know the perfect job for you," said Huey.

"You do?" asked Donald in surprise.

"Sure," said Dewey. "It's your old job with Uncle Scrooge."

"Why not?" said Louie. "You're great at asking Uncle Scrooge to hire you back."

Getting up all his courage, Donald walked into Uncle Scrooge's office.

"Uncle Scrooge, we need to talk!" he announced. "How would you like to hire back one perfectly trained assistant?"

"Fine," said Scrooge. "But no raise. Now get to work! These telephones have been ringing off the hook."

"Sure," said Donald. "Thanks. I think."

A few days later, Donald proudly gave Daisy her birthday present.

"Oh, Donald," Daisy gushed as she put on the necklace, "what a generous gift! How were you able to afford it?"

"It's all in day's work, Daisy," Donald laughed. "All in a day's work."